This book was first published in 1988 by Bracken Books
a division of Bestseller Publications Ltd
Princess House, 50 Eastcastle Street
London W1N 7AP, England

World Copyright, Text & Illustrations © Bracken Books, 1988

ISBN 1 85170 161 3

Printed and bound in Hungary

For my mother and father with love – J. H.

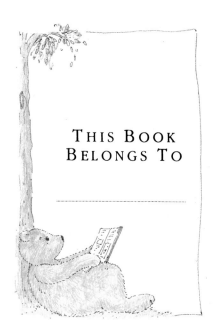

THIS BOOK
BELONGS TO

....

SNOW WHITE
— AND THE —
SEVEN DWARFS
AND OTHER TALES

ALI BABA AND THE FORTY THIEVES
THUMBELINA
JORINDA AND JORINDEL
A BOY ROBBING AN ORCHARD
THE MUSICIANS OF BREMEN
THE ANT AND THE PIGEON

RETOLD BY
GERALDINE CARTER

ILLUSTRATED BY
JANE HARVEY

BRACKEN BOOKS
LONDON

Snow White and the Seven Dwarfs

One cold winter's evening the queen of a
distant land sat by a window, sewing. The
frame of her window was made of the finest
black ebony, and as the queen gazed out at
the whirling snowflakes, the needle slipped
and pierced her finger. Three drops of bright
blood fell upon the snow outside.

"Ah," sighed the queen, "if only I could
bear a daughter with skin as white as the
snow, lips as red as my blood, and hair as
black as ebony." And soon afterwards, the
queen gave birth to a daughter whose skin
was as white as snow, whose lips were as red
as blood, and whose hair was as black as
ebony. She named the child Snow White,
but soon after the birth the queen herself
died.

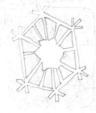

Before Snow White was a year old, the king took another wife. She was a fine-looking woman but also an extremely vain one. She even kept a magic looking-glass on the wall of her chamber and each morning she would stand before it and cry:

"Mirror, mirror, on the wall,
Who is the fairest of us all?"
And the mirror would reply:
"Thou, O Queen,
Art the fairest of the fair."
But, day by day, Snow White grew more beautiful and one morning when her stepmother gazed at the mirror and cried:
"Mirror, mirror, on the wall,
Who is the fairest of us all?"
it answered:
"Thou, O Queen, art so fair to see,
But Snow White is fairer far than thee!"

The Queen was outraged. She shook her mirror, turned green with envy, and screamed for a servant. As soon as the unfortunate servant arrived, she barked out her orders: "Take Snow White into a dark thick forest, and never let me look upon her face again! Return to me only with her heart."

The servant led Snow White into the depths of the forest, but the moment he drew his dagger to pierce her heart he found himself so touched by her beauty and gentleness that he dropped it to the ground. "Go without delay, or I will be forced to kill you, my child," he urged. Abruptly he turned his back on her and went on his way. After some time he killed a deer and removed its heart. That very evening he presented this heart to the evil queen.

As darkness fell in the forest, Snow White became very frightened, but at last she saw a light twinkling in the distance and ran towards it. There, beside an old oak tree, stood a dear little cottage.

Snow White peeped through the window and then crept inside. She was surprised to find that everything in the cottage was so small and spruce and neat. A low table was set with seven little plates and seven little loaves of bread, and Snow White nibbled each of the loaves in turn. But soon she felt so exhausted that she tumbled into one of the seven little beds lined up against the wall and fell fast asleep. Even when the door creaked open and seven dwarfs came bustling in she did not stir.

The dwarfs realised at once that something was wrong. *"Who has been eating my bread?" they cried* *in chorus. Then one of the dwarfs yelled: "Who is this sleeping in my bed?"* And all seven dwarfs rushed towards the bed. There lay Snow White, more beautiful than ever; they *oooohed* and they *aaaahed* and clicked their teeth, but they took care not to wake her up.

In the morning the dwarfs fussed around Snow White while she told them about her evil stepmother. They begged her to stay with them and asked her if she would clean and cook for them. "We shall take very good care of you," they cried in chorus. Of course Snow White agreed to stay for as long as they wished.

"We want you to stay with us for ever," said one of the dwarfs in a high, piping voice, and all the dwarfs nodded enthusiastically. "But mind you don't open the door to anyone," warned the dwarf with the deepest voice, "for it might be the queen herself come to kill you."

Snow White lived most happily with the dwarfs in their cottage. But after a while the queen confronted her mirror once again and cried:

"Mirror, mirror, on the wall,
Who is the fairest of us all?"

And it answered:

"Over the hills, beside an oak tree,
There dwells Snow White; 'tis true that she
Is fairer far, O Queen, than thee!"

The queen screamed with fury and turned white with spite. That very day she ventured out into the forest, disguised as a pedlar, and came at last the the dwarfs' cottage.

"Fine wares to sell! Laces and bobbins of all colours," she called as sweetly as she could.

Snow White peered out of the window: "Poor old thing, she looks quite worn out," she thought and she ran to the door to welcome the pedlar. "Please do come in," she said as she opened the door.

"You are too kind, my

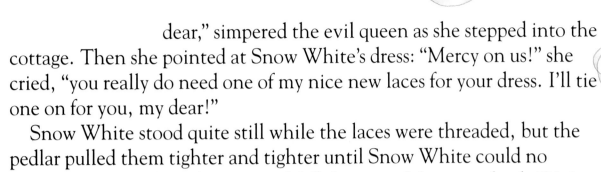

dear," simpered the evil queen as she stepped into the cottage. Then she pointed at Snow White's dress: "Mercy on us!" she cried, "you really do need one of my nice new laces for your dress. I'll tie one on for you, my dear!"

Snow White stood quite still while the laces were threaded, but the pedlar pulled them tighter and tighter until Snow White could no longer breathe. Then the poor girl fell down as if she were dead. "Ha! ha! ha!" cackled the queen, "let that be a lesson to you!", and she banged the door and hurried back to her palace.

In the evening when the seven dwarfs returned they saw Snow White lying on the floor, motionless. As they lifted her up and saw how tight the laces were pulled the tiniest dwarf rushed to fetch a pair of snippers. With great care, he sliced through the laces and soon Snow White began to breathe. The dwarfs sat in a circle around her as she told them all that had happened.

"Why, that was the queen herself, you silly child!" exclaimed the dwarf with the spotted suit. "Be more careful another time, or you might not be so lucky."

"Oh, surely she won't hurt me again!" cried Snow White. But she was wrong: the moment the queen returned home, she rushed to her mirror. And still the mirror answered her:

"*Over the hills, beside an oak tree,*
There dwells Snow White; 'tis true that she
Is fairer far, O Queen, than thee!"

The queen turned red with rage, and shook all over, when she heard these words. She flung on the clothes of an old servant woman, dipped her most precious comb in poison and returned to the forest.

"Fine wares! Fine wares!" she cried, outside the cottage door.

"Go away!" pleaded Snow White. "I dare not let you in."

"*Dare* not?" replied the queen. "What a funny girl. Why don't you let me show you some of my wares?" and so saying she stretched up her arm towards Snow White and handed her the poisoned comb.

The comb was so lovely and its jewels were so dazzling that Snow White could not resist running it through her long

black hair. No sooner had she
done so than the poison took effect
and she fell into a swoon.

"There you may lie," said the evil Queen
scornfully as she turned her back and went on her way.

When the seven dwarfs found Snow White lying as still as death
they rushed over to her and pulled the poisoned comb from her head
and Snow White slowly regained consciousness. They were so relieved
to see her open her eyes and to watch the color return to her cheeks,
that they quite forgot to be cross with her this time. But,
unfortunately, as soon as the queen returned to the palace she
confronted her mirror. When she received the same answer as before
her anger was great and she snarled at the mirror: "Snow White shall
die, if it costs me my life!"

The queen went to her secret hiding place and from there she
removed a juicy apple, rosy and shiny. She spent some time disguising
herself as a peasant and then she set off through the forest once more.

"Pretty lady!" she crooned when she arrived at the dwarfs' cottage,

"let me in, please. I have something for you!"

"The sooner you go away the better," replied Snow White nervously. "I know not who you are, but you must never take a step inside this house."

"Never mind," said the queen sweetly. "You need not be so sharp with me. Look, take this apple. It has a very special taste."

"N–no" said Snow White doubtfully, "I'd rather not."

"Silly girl! Do you think it is poisoned? See, you can have this half, and I will eat the rest." For this apple was so cunningly treated that only one side contained poison. When Snow White saw the old woman crunching the apple, she felt quite reassured and took a great bite out of her piece. As she swallowed it, she fell down dead.

"Nothing can save you now!" cried the queen. "My work is truly done." She ran back through the forest and when she reached the palace she went, at once, to her mirror. She was so breathless she could barely whisper the words:

"Mirror, mirror, on the wall,
Who is the fairest of us all?"

Now, at last, she heard the mirror proclaim the longed-for words:

"Thou, O Queen, art the fairest of all the fair."

When the dwarfs returned home and found Snow White, they were heartbroken. They could not understand how their beloved Snow White had been tricked again by the evil queen. "Why did she do it?"

they asked each other constantly, but they could find no answer to their question.

The dwarfs could not bear to hide Snow White in the cold stony ground; instead, they constructed a coffin of glass and carried it with great care into the hills. The dwarfs watched over her; day and night they took turns to keep vigil and Snow White was never left alone.

A long time passed but the dwarfs never gave up their vigil. One beautiful day a king's son came riding by and saw Snow White lying in her coffin. Death had not changed her in any way. She was still as white as snow, with lips as red as blood, and hair as black as ebony, and the prince fell in love with her immediately.

"You can have all my gold, everything I own, if you will but give me that coffin," he told the dwarfs, but they shook their heads.

"We love her too much," they said. "We cannot take your gold." But the prince was inconsolable and day after day he returned to be with Snow White. The dwarfs felt so sorry for the prince that after a time they agreed to let him take Snow White to his palace. As the king's son carefully lifted up the coffin, he tripped and jolted it.

Now a most strange thing happened, for that sharp knock caused the poisonous piece of apple to dislodge itself immediately

from Snow White's throat and after that she opened her eyes and started to breathe once more. The prince was overjoyed and at once he asked Snow White to marry him.

Many hundreds of people were invited to the wedding, including Snow White's wicked stepmother, for the king did not know that this woman was the evil queen.

On the day of the wedding itself the queen put on her very grandest clothes, and then she stood confidently and proudly before her looking glass:

> *"Mirror, mirror, on the wall,*
> *Who is the fairest of us all?"*

It replied:

> *"Thou, O Queen, art the fairest here I've seen;*
> *But fairer by far is the new-wed Queen."*

She snarled with rage when she heard these words, and as soon as she set eyes on the bride her rage and terror were too great to be borne.

Her eyes bulged, her blood turned to ice, she gave a terrible shriek and fell down dead.

Everyone was glad that the evil queen could cause no more harm and Snow White and her prince lived happily ever after. So, too, did her seven dear dwarfs.

Ali Baba and the Forty Thieves

Once upon a time, in Persia, there lived two brothers. The older of the two, Cassim, married a wealthy woman and became a rich merchant, but his younger brother, Ali Baba, married a woman just as poor as himself.

One day when Ali Baba was cutting wood at the edge of a forest he saw a great cloud of dust and as it came towards him he saw that the cloud was formed by a troop of horsemen. Sensing danger, he hid his donkeys in a thicket and clambered up into a tall tree.

The troop drew closer and closer until they stopped and dismounted right at the foot of the rock below Ali Baba's tree. He counted the men – forty there were – and he was frightened. The men's equipment, arms, and saddlebags were so heavy that the men could hardly lift them. "These bags must be full of silver and gold," thought Ali Baba. "Why else would they be so heavy?"

As he was wondering about the bags, something strange happened: the leader of the troop walked right up to the tree in which Ali Baba was crouching, pushed some shrubs to one side, and called in a loud voice: "Open, Sesame!"

At once a door opened right into the rock.

Ali Baba watched as the leader ordered his troops to enter inside.

He was so frightened that the men might emerge from the rock and discover him there, that he remained crouched in the tree.

After some time the door in the rock opened again. The leader appeared and stood outside counting his men as they dragged sacks out from the rock. "Close Sesame!" he called at last, and the rock door shut fast. Then, with much hustling and bustling, the troop heaved their sacks on to the horses and prepared to take their leave.

As they galloped out of the forest Ali Baba peered after them. No sooner were they out of sight than he climbed down from the tree and went straight to the hidden door. "Open Sesame!" he called. Instantly the door swung wide open and Ali Baba entered the cave. There he found, not the musty, dark cave he had expected to find but a large chamber stuffed full of silks, brocades and priceless carpets. He could see gold and silver bars piled up on the floor, and gold and silver coins lying strewn over the whole area. In a state of great excitement, Ali Baba rushed round the cave scooping up as much gold as he could carry in four large bags.

Ali Baba dragged his bags of gold to the door and called out: "Close Sesame!" Then loading up his donkeys, he covered the bags with wood, and returned to town.

Once inside his own home, he tipped up the bags, one by one, onto the floor. His wife could not believe her eyes and was amazed by Ali Baba's story. "I'll dig a hole and bury all this. There really isn't time to lose," he said finally.

"Yes, yes," she replied, "but, please, let's weigh the coins and see how rich we are." Before he could say yes or no, out of the door she ran, straight to Cassim's house to borrow a measure.

Now Cassim's wife was a meddling sort of woman and was mightily suspicious when she saw how excited her sister-in-law seemed. And so, before handing over the measure, she rubbed a little butter into the bottom of the bowl.

It took one whole hour for Ali Baba's wife to measure the gold he had brought from the cave. Then she returned to Cassim's wife with the measure and when Cassim's wife peered into the bowl, she noticed at once the glittering specks of gold stuck to the butter. That evening she challenged her husband: "Cassim, look how rich your brother is. He even measures his money, he's got so much!"

"What put such an absurd idea into your head?" said Cassim, roaring with laughter.

"It's true, it's true," protested his wife pointing to the gold glinting at the bottom of the measure.

Cassim peered into the bowl and turned green with envy. All that night he tossed and turned and in the morning, as the sun rose, he rushed to his brother's house. Through the door he burst, shouting: "Ali Baba, Ali Baba, why pretend to be so poor when you are measuring gold?" He pointed to the bottom of the bowl. Ali Baba smiled and nodded, and told his brother all

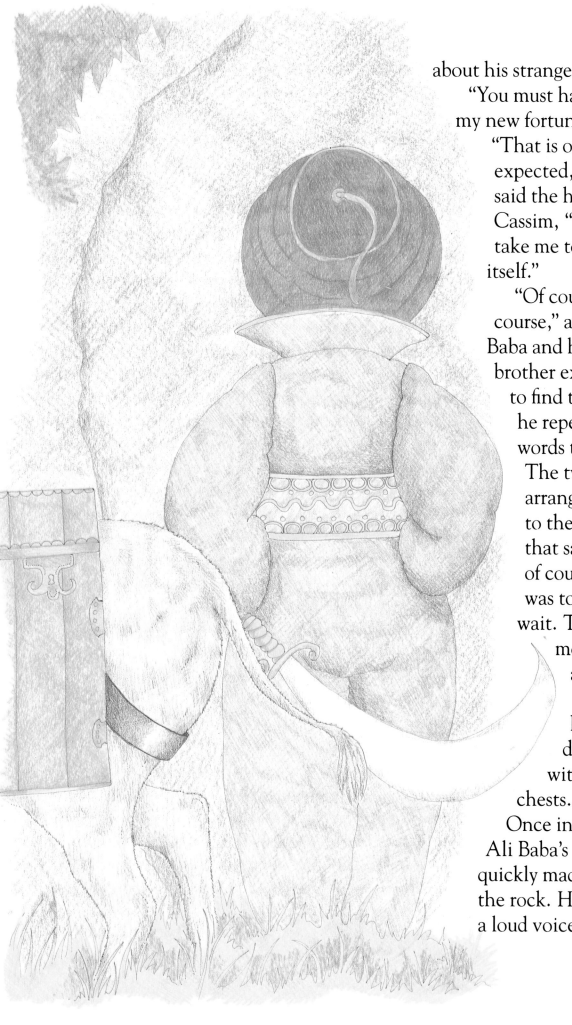

about his strange adventure. "You must have a share of my new fortune," he added.

"That is only to be expected, of course," said the haughty Cassim, "but you must take me to the cave itself."

"Of course, of course," agreed Ali Baba and he told his brother exactly where to find the rock. Then he repeated the pass words to Cassim.

The two brothers arranged to return to the rock later that same week, but of course Cassim was too greedy to wait. The following morning he rose at dawn and set out with his ten donkeys loaded with great empty chests.

Once in the forest, Ali Baba's brother quickly made his way to the rock. He called out in a loud voice: "Open,

Sesame!" and the door swung open. Cassim marched in, and called out: "Close Sesame!" Then he feasted his eyes on all the treasures that lay before him, and when he had collected together as much treasure as he could carry, he returned to the door. "Open Barley!" Nothing happened. "Open Corn!" he shouted even louder, "Open Wheat! Open Rice!" Still nothing happened. He had forgotten the password.

Before noon the robbers returned to the cave. They saw, at once, Cassim's donkeys roving about with empty chests on their backs and drew their swords. They stood in a circle around their captain as he called out: "Open, Sesame!" As the door of the rock swung open, Cassim leaped out and threw down the captain. But his action was in vain for the robbers attacked, killed and quartered him.

As night drew near, Cassim's wife grew uneasy and ran to Ali Baba's house to tell him that Cassim had gone to the cave. Ali Baba at once set out for the forest and later returned to town with his dead brother.

His brother's servant, Morgiana, opened the door to him. "This," said Ali Baba, "is the body of your murdered master. We must bury him as though he had died in his bed." Ali Baba then turned to comfort Cassim's wife and told her that he and his wife would come to live with her.

The following day Morgiana went to an apothecary and asked for some medicine. "My poor master," she said, "can neither eat nor speak, and no one knows what is the matter with him."
The very next day she returned to the apothecary, her eyes red from weeping, and asked for an essence given only to the dying. In the evening, therefore, no one was surprised to hear the wretched sounds of shrieking and crying coming from the house, nor to hear the announcement of

Cassim's death.

There was one more important task for Morgiana to carry out. At daybreak she approached Baba Mustapha, an old cobbler working near the gates of the town. She placed a piece of gold in his hand and asked him to follow her with his needle and thread. Then she bound his eyes with a handkerchief and led him through the town to the house of her dead master and to the very room where his body lay. She pulled off the cover, and ordered him to sew the quarters together and after the cobbler had completed his task, she blindfolded him and led him back to the market. Cassim was buried that same day.

The forty thieves, on their return to the cave, were much astonished to find that Cassim's body had vanished, together with some of their money bags. "Someone has found us," said the captain, "we are finished if we cannot discover that person. One of you must dress as a traveler and go

without delay into the city. Find out if there has been a strange and sudden death in the town."

One of the robbers disguised himself and entered the town at daybreak, just by Baba Mustapha's stall. The robber bade him good day, saying: "Honest man, how can you possibly see to stitch at your age?"

"Well, old as I am," replied the cobbler, "I do have very good eyes. Why, only yesterday, I sewed a dead body together in a pitch dark room."

The robber was overjoyed at his good fortune, and pressing a piece of gold into the cobbler's hand, begged him to lead him to the house where he had performed this remarkable deed. At first the cobbler refused, explaining how he had been blindfolded; but when the robber pressed more gold into his hand, he considered that he might possibly retrace his steps if blindfolded as before. And so, partly led, partly guided, the cobbler returned to Cassim's house. The delighted robber scored the mark of a cross on the door with a

piece of chalk, thanked the cobbler, and returned to report to his leader in the forest.

By and by Morgiana saw the mark and guessed that some mischief was afoot. With some chalk she boldly marked two or three more doors on each side and when the robbers finally reached the street, they were confronted by five or six crosses. Their guide was so puzzled he couldn't think what to say, and when the men returned to the forest he was at once beheaded.

The captain now decided to go himself, but when the stallholder led him to the house he did not mark the door. Instead he stared at it for a long, long time, making sure that he would recognize it on his return. That very day he ordered his men to go into the neighboring villages to buy nineteen donkeys and thirty-eight jars, and then to fill one only with oil.

The jars, all of them, were rubbed with oil and loaded onto the nineteen donkeys. Into each empty jar one man climbed. By dusk they had reached the town. The captain stopped his donkeys in front of Cassim's house and turning to Ali Baba, who was sitting outside, announced: "I have brought some oil from distant parts to sell at tomorrow's market, but it is now so late that I know not where to pass the night, unless you will do me the favor of taking me in." Ali Baba, who did not recognize the captain of the robbers in disguise, welcomed him warmly. Then he

opened his gates for the donkeys to enter, and
ordered Morgiana to prepare a bed and supper for his guest.

After they had supped, Ali Baba returned to the kitchen to speak to
Morgiana, and the captain walked out to the yard to give his men
instructions. "As soon as I throw stones from the window, lift up the lids
and climb out. I will be with you in a flash." Then he returned to the house
where Morgiana led him to his room.

As Morgiana cleared up in the kitchen, her lamp started to flicker. "Ah,
the oil from one of those jars will do," she thought. Out to the yard she
went but as she approached the first jar she heard, from inside that jar, a
voice whispering: "Is it time?"

Anyone else would have screamed, but Morgiana realized how much
danger her master was in, and answered: "Not yet, but soon." "Yes, yes,"
came the reply. To each jar in turn she went, repeating
the same words, and receiving the same answer until
she came to the last jar. No-one answered her and
so she lifted the lid, and saw that it was full of
oil. Now she knew what the robbers planned to
do. She filled her oil pot, quickly returned to
the kitchen and poured that oil into a kettle.
As soon as the oil started to bubble, she
returned to the yard, picked up each lid in
turn, and poured enough oil into every jar
to stifle and kill the robber inside. When
this brave deed was done, she put out
the fire and the lamp and waited in
darkness to see what would happen.

She did not have long to wait.
Soon the robber captain
opened the window and,
seeing that all seemed
quiet, aimed some little
pebbles at the jars. None
of his men stirred. He was
puzzled and so he decided to go
down into the yard to see what was
happening.

"Are you asleep?" he whispered as he approached the first jar, but as he smelled the horrible smell of burning oil he realized that his murderous plot had been discovered; his robbers were dead and now he must make his escape. Wasting not a moment, the robber captain scrambled over two walls and vanished.

At daybreak Ali Baba arose and, seeing the oil jars standing in the yard, asked why the merchant had not left with his donkeys. "Look in the first jar," Morgiana said and when Ali Baba did so he started back in terror. "Have no fear," said Morgiana, "the man cannot harm you; he is dead," and she told him the whole story.

The captain himself returned to the cave, which seemed lonely and frightening without his dead companions. "Ali Baba must be killed," he thought and so he set about making careful plans. First he disguised himself with cunning, and then he returned to town and took lodgings in an inn. Back and forth to the forest he went, carrying away as many rich materials and as much fine linen as he could. Then he opened a shop opposite the one belonging to Ali Baba's son.

Ali Baba's son was pleased to have such a rich merchant in his street and he invited his neighbor to dine at his father's house. When the merchant arrived, he told him that he had come to greet the father of his new friend but could not dine with them as he was forbidden to touch salted food. "If that is a problem," said Ali Baba, "let me assure you there shall be no salt in the food that we eat tonight."

Morgiana was surprised. "Who is this man," she said, "who eats no salt with his meat?"

"Do as I tell you, Morgiana," Ali Baba replied. But when the girl entered the dining room she recognized the robber captain in his disguise, so piercing

were his eyes. She saw, also, sticking out from a fold of his garment, the end of a dagger. When the dessert had been served, the robber captain was left alone with Ali Baba and his son. "When they are drunk I will kill then," he thought.

Morgiana hurriedly dressed herself in her dancing clothes and went to dance for Ali Baba's guest. Everyone was delighted, and after performing several dances, she held out her tambourine and the robber captain pulled out his purse to drop gold into it. But as he did so, Morgiana drew her dagger from its sheath and killed him.

"Morgiana!" cried Ali Baba "what have you done?"

"Master, he planned to kill you and your son. See here," she said, pointing to the captain's dagger, "see what an enemy you have entertained! He is both the false oil merchant and the captain of the forty thieves."

And now Ali Baba was so grateful he said: "You shall marry my son." And a few days later the wedding was celebrated with great splendor.

A year later, Ali Baba felt brave enough to return to the cave. The door opened when he called: "Open, Sesame!" and in he went. Nothing had been touched and Ali Baba carried away as much gold as he could. He told his son the secret of the cave, at last, and many years later his son was to hand down the secret to his children; and so the children and grandchildren of Ali Baba were rich to the end of their lives.

Thumbelina

Once upon a time there lived a woman who, more than anything in the world, longed for a tiny child. She had no idea where to get one, so she went to an old witch and asked: "Tell me, please, where I can get a tiny child? I do so long for one."

"Indeed, I can help you," said the witch before disappearing into her witch's hovel. She emerged seconds later clutching a sheath of corn. "Now this corn is quite, quite different from the corn which grows in the fields, or the chaff upon which chickens feed. Return home, plant it in a flower pot, and watch to see what happens."

"Thank you, thank you," said the woman excitedly as she handed twelve coins to the witch. She returned home and carefully planted the corn; and at once a large, statuesque flower emerged from the pot. Just like a tulip it looked, still in bud. "What a lovely flower" exclaimed the woman. She was so pleased that she kissed its pretty red and yellow petals – as she did so, the flower burst open with a loud snap. This was a real tulip, you could see that, but right in the middle of the flower, on its green stigma, sat a tiny girl, a lovely, delicate creature. She was not more than a thumb's height, and so she was called Thumbelina.

Thumbelina was given a cradle made from a glossy walnut shell and lined with petals of violets; a single rose leaf was her bed cover. At night she slept in the cradle, but throughout the day she played on the table. The woman had placed a large bowl of water on this table, and she surrounded the bowl with clusters of flowers, their stalks resting in the water. A large tulip petal floated on the water's surface, and on this petal sat little Thumbelina, sailing about from one side of the bowl to the other. She used two white horse hairs for her oars.

One night, as she lay in her pretty bed, a great, ugly toad jumped in through the window. Ugh! How hideous that huge, wet toad looked as she hopped down onto the table where Thumbelina lay sleeping under her rose leaf. "Here is a lovely wife for my son," croaked the toad as she spied the tiny sleeping creature. Grasping the walnut shell, she hopped away with it out through the window, into the garden.

A great broad stream ran past the bottom of the garden, and here on its swampy, muddy banks lived the toad with her son. "Let's put her on one of the big water lily leaves while we prepare the bridal chamber. She will be safe there," she croaked. And so the old toad took the walnut shell and swam to the water lily lying furthest from the shore. This was the biggest plant in the

whole stream. The toad placed Thumbelina on one of its giant leaves and there she left her.

When the tiny creature woke early in the morning and saw where she was, she began to cry most bitterly. Water lapped against every side of her big green leaf and she knew that there was no escape.

But the old toad was happy as she sat in the mud and busily decorated her ugly son's new home with grasses and buds of yellow water lilies. When the bridal home was ready, she and her son swam out to Thumbelina's water lily. The old toad curtseyed low in the water and announced:

"Here is my son, who is to be your husband. You will live together most comfortably in the mud."

"Croak, croak . . . kkkkkk," was all the son could say. Then the two toads took the pretty walnut cradle and swam away with it.

Thumbelina sat alone on the green leaf and wept, for she did not want the ugly fat toad to be her husband. The little fish swimming about in the water were so sorry to think of what lay in store for the tiny girl that they hatched a plan to rescue her. First they surrounded the green stem of her leaf, then they gnawed and gnawed at it with their teeth until it broke. Down the stream the leaf floated, carrying Thumbelina far away from the nasty toads and their muddy bank.

Thumbelina sailed further and further away until, at last, she reached a foreign land. There the countryside was beautiful and the sun shone on the water, making it look like liquid gold. A dainty white butterfly fluttered around the leaf and, at last, settled upon it. Thumbelina took her sash and tied one end of it around the butterfly, and the other end she fastened to the leaf. Then as the butterfly took off she glided through the water faster and faster.

But a big cockchafer caught sight of Thumbelina and in an instant he had fixed his legs round her slender waist and had flown off with her, up into a tree. The leaf

continued to float downstream and the butterfly, tied to that leaf, was unable to escape.

Heavens! How frightened poor little Thumbelina was when the cockchafer carried her up into the tree. But, more than anything, she grieved for the pretty white butterfly fastened to the leaf.

Of course the cockchafer cared nothing for Thumbelina's feelings. He settled with her on the largest leaf on the tree, and fed her with honey from the flowers. Although she was not a bit like a chafer he thought she was lovely; but when the other beetles kept telling him how ugly she was the cockchafer finally believed them, and then he wanted nothing more to do with Thumbelina.

The poor little girl lived quite alone in the wood all through the summer. She made a hammock of grass for herself and strung it up under a big dock leaf which gave her shelter from the rain. Thumbelina sucked the honey from the flowers, and drank the dew which lay on the leaves at sunrise. But, as winter drew near, all the birds which had sung so sweetly to her, flew away. The great dock leaf shrivelled up and Thumbelina was in danger of freezing to death. In the middle of winter the snow came and every single snow-flake which fell upon her felt like a shovelful of snow. She wrapped herself up in a withered leaf, but still she trembled with the cold.

Not far from the wood there was a large cornfield of bare, dry stubble, sticking up through the frozen ground. Thumbelina decided to leave the wood and as she walked through the cornfield, the stubble seemed to her like a forest. But still she shook with the cold. At last she stumbled upon the door of a field mouse's home, buried under the stubble. Behind that door she found a field mouse living cosily and warmly in her corn-filled room, with her kitchen and larder gleaming bright as can be. Thumbelina could not resist stepping inside the door and asking for a little piece of barley corn. "You poor little thing," the field mouse said, "come into my warm room and share my food. If you stay with me for the winter you can clean the house and tidy my room and tell me stories."

As soon as Thumbelina had settled down the field mouse told her: "Soon you will see my neighbor, for he comes to see me every day. He has a house that is even better than mine and he wears a most beautiful black velvet coat. If you can get him for a husband think how well off you will be. He can't see, so tell him all your best stories."

Thumbelina did not like the sound of this at all, for she knew that the field mouse's neighbor was a mole.

Soon the mole came to pay his visit. He listened most intently as the field mouse explained to Thumbelina that he was rich, and wise, and learned, but he had no liking for the sun or for beautiful flowers. Then she urged Thumbelina to sing to him. As she did so the mole fell in love with her, but he said not a word. He was a very discreet fellow. At this time the mole had just completed a long tunnel through the ground which connected the two houses, and he gave the field mouse and Thumbelina permission to walk through whenever

they liked. He warned them not to be frightened of the dead bird lying in the passage at the entrance to his tunnel. The mole led them through the long dark passage, holding in his mouth a piece of tinder wood which glowed like fire in the dark. Suddenly he thrust his broad nose into the roof, and pushed up the earth. Through the freshly made hole a shaft of daylight shone onto a dead swallow, wings pressed closely to its sides, legs and head drawn in under its feathers. Thumbelina felt real sorrow for the bird because she had come to love all the birds that had sung to her during the summer.

That night Thumbelina could not sleep, and so she got up out of her bed and braided a large rug out of hay. She carried it down to the tunnel and spread it over the dead bird. "Good-bye, you sweet bird," she whispered; but as she laid her head close to the bird's breast, she was startled by a thumping sound: it was the bird's heart.

The bird was not dead and now, revived by the warmth of the rug, it began to stir. Thumbelina quite shook with fright, for the bird seemed very large to her. But she gathered up her courage, tucked the rug closer around the creature, and fetched a leaf of mint to lay over his head. The next night she stole down again. The bird was live, but very weak and Thumbelina fetched water in a leaf to give to him. Then he told her how he had torn his wing on a blackthorn bush, and was not able to fly as fast as the other swallows. He had fallen to the ground at last. After that he remembered nothing.

The swallow stayed all winter in the tunnel with Thumbelina caring for him. She did not tell the mole or the field mouse anything, for they had no liking for the poor unfortunate bird.

As soon as spring came and the warmth of the sun penetrated the ground, the swallow said good-bye to Thumbelina. He asked her to travel with him, but Thumbelina knew how sad the old field mouse would be if she abandoned her. "No, I can't come with you," said Thumbelina sadly.

"Good-bye, good-bye, then, you kind girl," said the swallow as he flew out from the tunnel into the sunshine. "Tweet tweet," he sang as he soared up into the sky.

Thumbelina was very sad. She could not go out into the warm sunshine, for the corn, sown on the land near the field mouse's house, grew long and seemed like a dense forest to this poor little girl.

"You must work at your trousseau this summer," said the mouse to her, after their neighbor, the mole in the black velvet coat, had proposed marriage to her but Thumbelina did not care a bit for the tiresome mole.

Every morning at sunrise, and every evening at sunset, Thumbelina would steal out of the door and as the wind blew aside the tops of the cornstalks she would look at the blue sky, and think how seemed out there. She longed to see the dear didn't return.

Thumbelina's wedding outfit was ready. "In bright and lovely it swallow again but he

When autumn came. four weeks you must be married," the field mouse announced. But Thumbelina cried and said that she would not have the tiresome mole for a husband.

"Fiddle-dee-dee," said the field mouse, "you should thank heaven for such a husband!"

The day of the wedding came and the mole arrived to take Thumbelina to live deep down under the ground. The poor child was heartbroken at the thought of bidding good-bye to the beautiful sun. As she walked out of the field mouse's house, she turned to a little red flower: "Please give my love to the dear swallow if you happen to see him," she said.

"Tweet . . . tweet." the swallow himself was passing just above her head and when she told him about the ugly mole, and how she was to live deep down underground, he asked her to fly with him. Come with me. Sit on my back and tie yourself on with your sash and we can fly far away, to a warm country where the sun always shines.

Thumbelina tied a ribbon around a strong feather, and they flew away, high up into the air above forest and lakes and great mountains.

At last they reached the warm country where the sun shone with a powerful glow, where beautiful green and blue grapes grew in clusters on the hedgerows, and orange and lemon trees filled the woods. As the swallow flew on, the country grew more beautiful. They saw, by the shore of the blue sea, a dazzling white marble palace, vines twined round its ancient pillars. "Here is my house," said the swallow, "choose any one of the gorgeous flowers growing down there and I will place you on it."

A great marble column lay on the ground in three broken pieces, with lovely white flowers clustered around. The swallow flew down and placed Thumbelina upon one of their broad leaves and, to her great astonishment, there was a tiny man in the middle of the flower, bright and transparent, as if made of glass with a sparkling golden crown on his head. "How beautiful he is," whispered Thumbelina to the swallow.

The little prince was delighted, for Thumbelina was quite the prettiest girl he had ever seen.

He placed his crown on her head, and asked her to be his wife and queen of the flowers! A little lady or gentleman emerged from each flower, bearing gifts for Thumbelina. A large white butterfly gave her a pair of pretty wings. Now as she flew from flower to flower everyone rejoiced except for the swallow who sat alone in his nest. He was so fond of Thumbelina that he did not wish to part from her.

"Good-bye, good-bye," he sang when at last he left the warm country, and flew back to his homeland. There he had a little nest above a window of the house where the man who wrote this story lived, and there he sang his "tweet . . . tweet" to the man, and so we have the story of Thumbelina.

Jorinda and Jorindel

Once upon a time there was an old castle that stood in the
middle of a large dense wood, and in that castle there lived a
bad fairy. All day long she flew about in the form of an owl, or
crept stealthily around in the form of a cat,
but at night she became an old woman
again. Whenever any young man walked
within a hundred paces of her

castle, he became quite fixed, unable to move a step until she came to set him free; but when any young girl came within that distance, she was changed into a bird, and placed in a cage which was then hung in a castle chamber. There were seven hundred of these cages in the castle, and every single one contained a beautiful bird.

Now there was, at that time, a young girl whose name was Jorinda and she was the prettiest girl imaginable. Jorinda was engaged to a shepherd named Jorindel and soon they were to be married.

One evening Jorinda and Jorindel went for a walk in the wood and as they strolled along Jorindel warned: "We must take care not to go too close to the castle." It was a beautiful evening, with the last rays of the setting sun shining brightly through the long branches of the trees onto the green undergrowth. Turtledoves were singing their plaintive songs from the tall birch trees.

Jorinda and Jorindel sat down to rest, but all of a sudden they were overcome by sadness; they could think of no reason for their melancholy but felt strongly that they were about to be parted for ever.

By that time they had wandered right into the wood and, when they looked for the way home, they could not find their path. The sun was setting fast, disappearing beneath the horizon, and when Jorindel looked behind him he saw, through the bushes, the walls of the old castle. Jorindel shrank back in fear, turned pale, and trembled. Jorinda was singing a melancholy song:

"The ring-dove sang from the willow spray,

Well-a-day!
Well-a-day!
He mourned
For the fate
Of his lovely mate,
Well-a-day!"

Abruptly the singing ceased. Jorindel turned towards her and as he did so Jorinda changed into a nightingale, and her song ended with a mournful cry. An owl with fiery eyes flew round them three times screaming: "Tu whit! Tu whu! Tu whit! Tu whu!" Jorindel could not move. He stood fixed as a stone, neither able to weep, nor to speak, nor could he stir hand or foot. And now, as the sun went down, the gloomy night closed all around him and the owl flew into a bush.

A moment later, the bad fairy came forth pale and wasted, with staring eyes, and a nose and chin that almost met one another. She mumbled to herself, seized the nightingale, and disappeared through the trees with the bird in her hand. Poor Jorindel saw everything but what could he do? He was fixed to the spot unable to move.

At last the fairy returned and called out with her rasping voice:

"Till the prisoner's fast,
And her doom is cast,
There stay!
Oh, stay!
When the charm is around her,
And the spell has bound her,
Hie away! away!"

Jorindel, finding that he was free, fell on his knees before the fairy, and begged her to give him back his dear Jorinda. "You will never set eyes on her again," she retorted, and with those words turned on her heels

and departed.

Jorindel prayed and he wept: "Alas!" he said, "what is to become of me?" As he could not return to his own home he went instead to a strange village where he found work as a shepherd. Many times he returned to the woods and walked round and round the castle, as close to it as he dared to go. One night he dreamed that he had found a beautiful purple flower, and in the middle of that flower there lay a priceless pearl. In his dream Jorindel plucked the flower and carried it in his hand right into the castle. There everything he touched with the flower became disenchanted, and there, at last, he found his dear Jorinda again.

In the morning when he awoke, he began looking for the purple flower. Eight long days he sought for it in vain; but on the ninth day, early in the morning, he found the beautiful flower in whose center lay a drop of dew as large as a precious pearl.

Jorindel plucked the flower, and set out for the castle. Night and day he traveled until he came to within sight of the fortress. He walked closer to it than a hundred paces, and yet he did not become fixed as before, but found that he was able to approach the castle door.

Jorindel was very glad. He touched the door with the flower, and watched as it sprang open. Through the court he went and as he walked right into the castle he heard the singing of hundreds of birds. At last he came to the chamber where the fairy sat, with the seven hundred birds singing in their seven hundred cages.

When the fairy saw Jorindel she was furious, and screamed with rage, but she could not come

within two yards of
him; for the purple
flower he held in his hand
protected him.

He looked around at the birds, but
how amongst so many nightingales could
he find his Jorinda? He examined one
cage after another but all the birds
seemed alike to him and all of them had
stopped singing. While he was thinking
what to do, the fairy rushed past him and
unlocked one of the cages. Then she
made her escape through the door.
Jorindel ran after her, and he touched
the cage with the delicate purple flower.
There, in an instant, stood his Jorinda
looking as beautiful as ever, as lovely as
the day when they had walked together
in the wood.

Then Jorindel went to each cage in
turn and gently touched all the other
birds with the flower; and they at once
resumed their old forms.

Jorindel then led his dear Jorinda
home, and they lived happily together
for many years.

A Boy
Robbing
an Orchard

Once upon a time there lived a greedy
young boy called Tom. He was
strutting along the road one day
when he came upon a large
orchard full of fine trees. Now
it was a whole hour until lunch
time, and Tom was feeling
exceedingly hungry. He glanced up
at the trees, laden with beautiful red
apples; they looked so juicy
and tempting that his
mouth started to water.
"Why, there are *hundreds*
of trees in that orchard, all
covered in apples," he
said to himself.
"Who would grudge
me one or two?

No-one will even notice."

So he hopped over
the wall, and in a trice he was scrambling up
the nearest tree. Up and up he climbed,
munching at a small apple on the way, until
he reached the really rosy apples at the top.
  Tom was sitting high up in the tree
stuffing himself to his heart's content,
when he heard a sudden shout from
below. Glancing down, he saw a very

angry man brandishing his walking stick at the tree.

"*Hey!* keep your thieving hands off my apples!" cried the furious man. "Come down from there at once, you little devil!"

"Come and make me!" spluttered Tom between mouthfuls.

"Well, I'd sooner *you* came down to me. But if you won't come down of your own free will, then there'll be nothing to do but to make you. They say there is great virtue in herbs and suchlike; they'll teach you a lesson!" And so saying the old man stooped down, plucked a handful of grass and hurled it up at the boy.

Tom roared with laughter as the grass wafted gently downwards in the

wind.

"Good try, mister!" he jeered. "Better luck next time!"

"I reckon I *shall* have better luck next time," retorted the old man. "For if grass is no use, then I shall try stones."

And that is exactly what he did and Tom, battered and bruised and sore from head to toe, never stole anything else in his life.

The Musicians of Bremen

Once upon a time there lived a donkey who had served his master faithfully for many long years. But now he was growing old, and every day he became less and less fit for hard work. The donkey's master became impatient and planned to do away with him, but the crafty animal could see that some mischief was afoot. He decided to take himself off and so he began the long journey towards the great city: "For there," thought he, "I will become a musician."

The donkey had traveled only a little way along the path when he spied a dog lying by the roadside, panting hard as if he were very tired.

"What makes you pant so, friend?" asked the donkey in surprise.

"Alas!" replied the dog, "now that I am old and weak, and can no longer keep up with the hunt, my master decided to knock me on the head; so I ran away. But however can an old dog like me earn a living?"

"Why, I myself am going to the great city to become a musician!" exclaimed the astonished donkey. "Why don't you come along too?"

The dog was quite delighted with the offer, and off they trotted together. But before long they caught sight of a most miserable-looking cat sitting in the middle of the road.

"Why, my good cat, is something wrong?" inquired the donkey. "You look quite out of spirits!"

"Indeed! So would you, if your life was in danger!" mewed the cat indignantly. "Simply because I am no longer young, and prefer to lie in comfort by the fire, rather than run about the house chasing mice, my mistress grabbed hold of me and was going to *drown* me! I escaped just in time, but I don't know how I am to make a living."

"You are *most* welcome to come along with us," said the donkey. "I've heard you caterwauling to the moon many a night, and there's no doubt you will make a fine musician."

So on they went, until they came to a farmyard with a big, handsome cock perched upon the gate. He was screeching out with all his might and main.

"Bravo!" cried the donkey. "Upon my word what a splendid noise; but what is it all about?"

"Why, I was just saying that we should have fine weather for our washing-day, but do I get thanked for my pains? Indeed not! Instead, my mistress and the cook threatened to cut off my head, and turn me into broth for their guests!"

"Heaven forbid!" brayed the donkey, "do come with us, master Chanticleer. It will be better, at any rate, than staying here to have your head chopped off! Besides, who knows? With a bit of luck, we four could perform some kind of concert in the great city."

And so the donkey, the dog, the cat and the cock went merrily on their way.

At twilight they stopped to rest beside a great oak tree, since

they had no chance of reaching the
great city that night. The donkey
and the dog lay down under the tree; the cat climbed into the branches;
and the cock, thinking that the higher he was, the safer he'd be, flew
right to the very top of the tree. The cock peered all around, as he
usually did before settling down each night. Suddenly he caught a
glimpse of something shining in the distance. "There must be a house
over there, for I can see a light!" the cock called down to his
companions.

"If that is so,'" said the cat, "let's hurry off there, for this tree is mighty
uncomfortable!"

"Besides," added the dog, "I certainly wouldn't mind a juicy big bone
or two."

So the travelers set off towards the light; and as they grew nearer, it
became larger and brighter until at last they reached a house, which was
inhabited by a whole gang of robbers.

The donkey, being the tallest of the company, marched up to the
window and peeped in. "Well," said Chanticleer impatiently, "what do
you see?"

"What do I see?" repeated the donkey. "Why, I see a table spread with
delicious food, and robbers sitting round it making merry.

That house would make a perfect home for us, if only we could get in."

So the friends put their heads together and planned how they might drive the robbers out, and at last they came up with a plan. The donkey stood upright on his hind-legs, with his fore-feet resting against the window; the dog clambered up onto his back; the cat scrambled up onto the dog's shoulders; and the cock flew up and perched upon the cat's head. Then the donkey brayed, the dog barked, the cat mewed, and the cock crowed; and suddenly they all smashed through the window together, and tumbled into the room with a hideous clatter! The robbers, who had been quite terrified by the "concert", were certain that some frightful hobgoblin had burst in upon them. Without stopping for a second glance, they leaped up and scampered away as fast as their legs would carry them.

The delighted travelers were soon sitting down and tucking into the feast as heartily as if they had not eaten for a month. Then each of them went to look for a resting place.

The donkey lay down on a heap of straw in the yard; the dog stretched out on a

mat behind the door; the cat curled up on the hearth in front of the glowing ashes; and the cock perched up upon the rafters. Soon they were all fast asleep.

But when the robbers saw from afar that the lights were out and that all seemed quiet, they began to wonder if, after all, they had been in too great a hurry to get away. The chief robber, bolder than the rest, went marching back to the house to see what was going on. Finding everything still, he crept into the kitchen, and groped about for a match to light the candles. When he saw the glittering fiery eyes of the cat, he mistook them for live coals, and held out the match to light them. In a fury, the cat sprung at his face, spitting and hissing and scratching. Shrieking with terror, the robber dashed for the back door, only to wake the dog, who bit a good chunk out of his leg. He fled across the yard where the donkey aimed a great kick at him, while the cock, who had been woken by all this noise, crowed away for all he was worth.

The robber sped back to his companions and told them how a fearsome witch who was lurking in the house had spat at him and scratched his face with her long bony fingers; how a man had hidden behind the door, and stabbed him in the leg; how a black monster had stood in the yard and struck him with a club; and how the devil himself had sat upon the top of the house and cried out: "Throw the rascal up here!"

Hearing this, the robbers trembled from head to foot, and never dared to return to the house. But the delighted musicians decided to stay in the house for good; and there they are to this very day.

The Ant and the Pigeon

Once upon a time there lived a glossy black ant who, one fine summer's day, traveled further than usual from her nest. After a long journey she found herself, at midday, by the edge of a small stream. "What good fortune," thought the ant, for by this time, after such a tiring journey, she was feeling decidedly thirsty. "First of all I'll have a drink and then, after that, I'll take a nap," she thought. She leaned far, far out over the water's edge, but in her eagerness she leaned a little *too* far out, and she found herself tumbling head over heels into the stream. "Help! Help! Save me!" she screamed desperately as she plunged into the water. But, at this time of day, there were few creatures around, and those who did hear her cries just shrugged their shoulders and said: "Oh well, it's only an ant. Who cares whether an ant

lives or dies!"
But there was one creature who
did hear the cries of the poor little ant
and who did take pity on her. A beautiful wood
pigeon happened to be flying directly over the
stream at that moment and saw all that had
happened. She did not hesitate for a second.
Swooping down, she took hold of a twig in

her beak and dropped it into the water, right in front of the ant. The grateful ant seized hold of the twig and clung on to it with all her might, and thus she was saved from drowning.

Of course, the ant never forgot that she owed her very life to the kind and quick-thinking pigeon. She longed to repay her, but how could the services of a mere ant be of any use to a bird? One day, as the ant wandered through the countryside, she came upon a man who was aiming his gun

at the very pigeon who had saved
her life! Without a second's hesitation, the
ant ran up to the man and stung him hard
on the ankle.
   "Aaaaaaaaahhhhhh!" roared the man,
as he dropped his gun, clasped his injured
ankle and started hopping about on one foot.
The horrible noises made by the hunter so startled
the wood pigeon that she leapt into the air,
flapped her wings and flew off
to safety.
   And so, at last, the
little ant was able
to show gratitude
to the kind pigeon
who had saved her life.